JO...

GW00857887

JOSHUA JONES

MRS KARIA

# MEET ALL THESE FRIENDS IN BUZZ BOOKS:

Thomas the Tank Engine
The Animals of Farthing Wood
Fireman Sam
Joshua Jones
Rupert
Babar
James Bond Junior

First published in Great Britain 1993 by Buzz Books,
an imprint of Reed Children's Books
Michelin House, 81 Fulham Road, London, SW3 6RB
and Auckland, Melbourne, Singapore and Toronto

Joshua Jones film © copyright 1990 S4C/Channel 4 Wales
Joshua Jones character © copyright 1989 Rob Lee
Text © copyright 1993 Reed International Books Limited
Illustrations © copyright 1993 Reed International Books Limited
Based on the animation series produced by Bumper Films
for S4C/Channel 4 Wales and Prism Art & Design Limited
Produced and directed by Ian Frampton and John Walker
Photographs by John Walker

ISBN 1 85591 236 8

Printed in Italy by Olivotto

# NIGHT WATCH

Story by Olivia Madden
Developed from a script
by Bob Wilson

One fine morning, Fiona was down at Clattergate Farm helping Mr Laski. Daphne Peacock, the vet, was there too. Trojan, Mr Laski's horse, had a sore hoof.

"Ah, here's the culprit," said Daphne, removing a piece of metal. "Hold him steady, Fi, while I put on some ointment."

Over in the sty, the pigs were squealing
noisily and poking their snouts through
the fence.

"What's the matter with them today, Joe?"
asked Daphne.

"They are hungry. I'm waiting for a special
delivery of pig food. Josh will bring it soon,"
explained Mr Laski.

Joshua Jones arrived at Sharon's café to find Spanner and Ravi having a snack.

"I'm exhausted," Spanner was saying. "I've just been fixing up a burglar alarm for Wilton Cashmore. A highly sensitive and sophisticated system."

"A bit like you, eh Spanner?" teased Josh.
"I'm on my way to Joe Laski's with his pig
feed, Ravi. Do you want to come with me?"

"Oh, yes please!" Ravi replied.

Josh chugged up the canal towards Clattergate Farm.

"Any sign of Joe, Ravi? He said he'd meet us with the tractor," said Josh.

"I can see Joe and Fiona," said Ravi, "but no tractor. Joe's wheeling a pram."

"A pram. That sounds odd."

Josh moored by Joe's bottom field. "What's up, Joe?" he called.

"Oh Josh. So sorry. We will use the pram to move sacks. I have no diesel for the tractor."

"I've a spare can on board. Have that."

"Thank you, no. I have spent all my money on the pigs. We will manage fine like this."

Meanwhile, Wilton was showing off his new burglar alarm.

"It's *very* sensitive, Mrs Karia. One hint of a burglar and off it goes," he said, crossing over to the window to demonstrate.

Immediately the alarm began to flash and a shrill ringing noise pierced the air.

"How do you switch it off, Mr Cashmore?" shouted Mrs Karia, clapping her hands over her ears.

"I don't know," wailed Wilton. "I'll have to get Spanner."

13

"It's probably what we experts call a shortened circular," said Spanner.

"I don't care what it is," shrieked Wilton. "Just shut it up."

"Right you are," said Spanner.

He took a large hammer from his tool kit.

"This'll do the trick," he said.

Spanner gave the alarm box a whack, and
the ringing stopped immediately.

"I'll leave you the hammer, Mr C, in case
it goes temperamental again," he offered.

It was hard work wheeling a pram full of pig food up the track to the farmyard.

"We leave the rest for now," said Joe, "and put it in the barn later."

"Not worried about Mad Jack then?" teased Josh.

Ravi pricked up his ears. "Mad Jack? Who's he?"

"It's a very old story," said Joe. "Mad Jack was a robber long ago who hid a treasure in my barn. People say he comes haunting once a year."

"Golly," said Fiona. "A ghost! When does he come?"

"On the night of June 13th," grinned Josh.

"That's tonight!" Ravi exclaimed.

Wilton had a headache. He lay on the settee while Mrs Karia dusted quietly. Suddenly the telephone rang. Wilton jumped up and ran outside to the balcony.

"Hello, Mr Laski," said Mrs Karia. "Yes, Ravi may stay at the farm tonight. One moment, I'll ask about Fiona." Mrs Karia went onto the balcony. "Mr Cashmore...Mr Cashmore, what are you doing with that hammer?"

"I've had enough of this alarm!" he shouted.

"But Mr Cashmore," said Mrs Karia, " that was the telephone ringing..."

Too late. The alarm was off the wall and in pieces in Wilton's hands.

Mrs Karia returned to the telephone. "I think it's a fine idea for Fiona to stay at the farm," she told Mr Laski.

Josh sat on the deck of the *Delilah* drinking a cup of cocoa in the moonlight.

"Joe Laski's a stubborn old sausage, isn't he, Fairport? If he'd let me put some diesel into his tractor, we'd be finished by now."

Suddenly, Josh smiled. "Fairport, that's given me an idea."

"Come on, Ravi. It's getting late. Time to check out the ghost," said Fiona.

The children tiptoed downstairs and pushed open the heavy front door of the farmhouse.

As they crossed the yard to the barn, an owl screeched.

"It's a bit creepy here," Ravi whispered.

"Don't be silly," Fiona said. "Let's find somewhere to hide. How about the hayloft?"

"After you then," said Ravi.

"Come on. There's no such thing as ghosts, you know," Fiona told him.

Reluctantly, Ravi climbed the ladder. Some hay brushed against his leg. Ravi shivered. As he reached the top, the barn door banged and a dark figure appeared in the doorway, silhouetted in the moonlight.

"It's the ghost," gulped Ravi.

"Quick, hide!" whispered Fiona.

They watched the figure cross the barn and then switch on a torch.

"Ghosts don't have torches, do they?" asked Ravi.

"He's stealing Joe's tractor. Let's get him," said Fiona. "1, 2, 3 — JUMP!"

With a whoop, the children landed in a pile of straw on top of the mysterious figure. The figure yelled and struggled to escape.

"Mr Laski! Help us," cried Ravi.

Joe Laski was dreaming peacefully when he was woken by shrieks coming from the barn. He grabbed his torch and ran out across the courtyard.

"What's all this blinkin' racket?" he shouted.

"We've caught a burglar," cried Fiona.

"Let's see who he is. Pull that sack away from his face," said Joe.

"Oh dear!" cried Ravi, Fiona and Joe in unison. "It's Josh!"

"That's the last time I try to do you a favour, Joe," grinned Josh. "It's far too dangerous."

When Daphne Peacock arrived the next morning to inspect Trojan's hoof, she found Joe and Josh unloading pig food.

"There. All done in one go," said Josh.

"Thank you so much, Josh. And you too, children," said Joe. "You're all very brave."

"Very brave?" said Daphne.

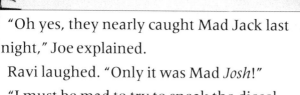

"Oh yes, they nearly caught Mad Jack last night," Joe explained.

Ravi laughed. "Only it was Mad *Josh*!"

"I must be mad to try to sneak the diesel into Joe's barn with you two around," Josh replied. "You're better protection than Mr Cashmore's burglar alarm!"

**SPANNER**

**FAIRPORT**

**FIONA CASHMORE**     **RAVI KARIA**